Cartoon

by

Steve Yockey

MUSIC USE NOTE

Licensees are solely responsible for obtaining formal written permission from copyright owners to use copyrighted music in the performance of this play and are strongly cautioned to do so. If no such permission is obtained by the licensee, then the licensee must use only original music that the licensee owns and controls. Licensees are solely responsible and liable for all music clearances and shall indemnify the copyright owners of the play and their licensing agent, Samuel French, Inc., against any costs, expenses, losses and liabilities arising from the use of music by licensees.

IMPORTANT BILLING AND CREDIT REQUIREMENTS

All producers of *CARTOON must* give credit to the Author of the Play in all programs distributed in connection with performances of the Play, and in all instances in which the title of the Play appears for the purposes of advertising, publicizing or otherwise exploiting the Play and/or a production. The name of the Author *must* appear on a separate line on which no other name appears, immediately following the title and *must* appear in size of type not less than fifty percent of the size of the title type.

In addition the following credit *must* be given in all programs and publicity information distributed in association with this piece:

The World Premiere of ***CARTOON*** opened April 1, 2006 at 7 Stages in Atlanta, GA. Produced by Out of Hand Theater with Co-Producing Artistic Directors Ariel de Man, Adam Fristoe and Maia Knispel, and Managing Director Kathleen Donahoe. Directed by Adam Fristoe.

Scenic Design . . . . Jimmy Hilburn
Lighting Design . . . . .Neil Anderson
Sound Design . . . . Rene Dellefont
Costumes Design . . . . Carrie Duncan

ESTHER . . . . .Maia Knispel
TROUBLE . . . . .Brian Crawford
WINSTON PUPPET . . . . Geoff Uterhardt
AKANE . . . . .Ariel de Man
YUMI . . . . Angela Porter
SUITOR . . . . .Theroun Patterson
DAMSEL . . . . Rebecca Dutton
ROCK STAR . . . . .Joe Sykes
VOLUNTEER . . . . .Nick Strangis

The West Coast Premiere of ***CARTOON*** opened February 2, 2007 at La Val's Subterranean in Berkeley, CA. Produced by Impact Theatre with Artistic Director Melissa Hillman and Managing Director Cheshire Isaacs. Directed by Mark Routhier.

Scenic Design . . . . .Stephanie Buchner
Lighting Design . . . . Jon Nagel
Sound Design . . . . David Guilmette
Costume Design . . . . Choco Couture Costuming

ESTHER . . . . Erika Salazar
TROUBLE . . . . .Jeremy Forbing
WINSTON PUPPET . . . . Chris Yule
AKANE . . . . Molly Anne Coogan
YUMI . . . . Helen Nesteruk
SUITOR . . . . .Jon Lutz
DAMSEL . . . . Marissa Keltie
ROCK STAR . . . . .Joseph Rende
VOLUNTEER . . . . Joshua Huston, Jon Nagel, Chuck Phelps
                                                                    Brian Turner

LIST OF PLAYERS

TROUBLE – A cute, mischievous young man, an idealist

ESTHER – A bossy little girl with an old-fashioned microphone, a bad temper, and a big imagination

WINSTON PUPPET – A puppet with strings

SUITOR – A hopeful boy clown

DAMSEL – A bashful girl clown

YUMI – A mischievous Anime school girl

AKANE – A mischievous Anime school girl

ROCKSTAR – A heartthrob giant stuffed animal with claws

VOLUNTEER – A hapless volunteer from the audience

SETTING

The floor curves into the back wall, which is painted sky blue with white clouds. A thick rope hangs from the ceiling stage center. One large, bright red, overstuffed armchair is present. There is a small table next to the chair with an unrealistically proportioned, old-fashioned alarm clock. The floor is covered with stuffed animals and toys of differing shapes and sizes. All props should be carried on and off by characters as needed.

AUTHOR"S NOTE:

[ ] in the script indicate overlapping dialogue.

<< >> in the script indicate portions of Esther's dialogue amplified through a microphone.

The Suitor and Damsel are tacit for the entire play unless noted

Episode titles should be incorporated (signs, ring cards, etc)

Characters that die remain dead on stage through the curtain call

In performance, the Cartoon Theme Song should be very rhythmic, hands clapping, feet pounding; like the most sugar shocked of Saturday morning cartoons; bright, infectiously zany and infused with an "on with the show" breakneck speed. Especially as it's performed all the way through twice.

Theme Song

(The playing space is a three quarter thrust sloping up into the back wall in the rear and corners. Seating is in banks, studio style. The back wall is a bright depiction of blue sky and white clouds. There is a large "APPLAUSE" sign hanging from the ceiling. The floor of the entire space is covered with stuffed animals and toys. A rope hangs from the ceiling that presumably leads up into the lighting grid. A large red armchair is present with a side table supporting a ridiculously oversized alarm clock. A ridiculously oversized sledgehammer leans against the chair.)

*(***CHARACTERS*** enter, fall into position...)*

*(All characters are present, asleep on the stage and in the audience. **ESTHER** is in the armchair, the **ROCKSTAR** is asleep curled up at her feet, the **WINSTON PUPPET** is suspended on the wall with ropes leading up into the air, the **SCHOOL GIRLS** lean against each other, the **SUITOR** and **DAMSEL** are as far apart as possible.)*

*(The alarm clock goes off. It rattles on the table, a deafening ring. Everyone covers their ears or heads groaning as **ESTHER** gropes around for her hammer. She grabs it, holds it to her as everyone springs to life.)*

Song – "CARTOON THEME SONG"

GROUP.

CARTOOOOOOON! CARTOOOOOOON!
(slide whistle up)
Let's go!

This is Trouble. He causes so much Trouble.

If you see him coming, you should tell us on the double,
'Cause he's trouble, "Yes I am!"
He'll burst your bubble, "Yes I will!"
That's trouble with "T"
and that rhymes with "P"
and that stands for…

TROUBLE.

"positively adorable"

(There is a collective groan.)

ESTHER. Take it girls!

GROUP.

Akane and Yumi.
Two schoolgirls who have
G-r-e-a-t-h-a-i-r "Great Hair!"
L-i-p-g-l-o-s-s *(kiss sound)* "Lip Gloss!"
A-K-A-N-E-Y-U-M-I BEST FRIENDS!
B-e-s-t-f-r-i-e-n-d-s BEST FRIENDS!

(There is frantic clap choreography during the upcoming "Whoa:")

WHOOOOOOOOOOAAAAAAAUp Next!

Rockstar! Rockstar is so cool. You. Won't. Know what to do,
You'll stand there. In a trance. While He. Is mauling you.
Rockstar!
"Rahr"

(The girls swoon and faint…)

And now…

He frowns a lot, he sighs a lot, but mostly he just hangs there,
Winston Puppet…It's Winston Puppet…
Sometimes he'll sing, sometimes he'll dance, but mostly he just hangs there,
Winston Puppet…

WINSTON PUPPET.

I'm Winston Puppet.

(There is a collective sigh.)

GROUP.

Bam! Love Explosion!
Suitor, never gets what he wants
Damsel, never gets what she wants
Suitor never gets what he wants
Which is the Damsel

Damsel, never gets what she wants
Suitor, never gets what he wants,
Damsel, never gets what she wants
Which is the Suitor

Love, doesn't make any sense
Love, doesn't make any sense
"Nobody"
                              "Nobody"
                                   "Nobody"
                                        "Nobody"

Nobody gets – what they want

Cartoooooon! Cartoooooon!
(Slide whistle down)

ESTHER. "Now me!"

GROUP.
And then there's Esther, she's in charge
She's kind of small –

ESTHER.
"But very large!"

GROUP.
She's kind of loud –

ESTHER.
"Hey, watch it!"

GROUP.
She's kind of mean –

ESTHER.
"I'm warning you!"

GROUP & ESTHER.
She's always right.
       "I'm always right!"
She's always right.
       "I wrote this song!"
She's always right.
 "I'm always right."

*(***ESTHER*** *slams down the hammer to punctuate the song, everyone is knocked off their feet and falls back to sleep.)*

(Pause. Day becomes night, becomes day in a matter of moments.)

(The alarm clock goes off again. It rattles on the table, a deafening ring. Everyone covers their ears or heads groaning as **ESTHER** *gropes around for her hammer. She grabs it, holds it to her as everyone springs to life.)*

Song – "CARTOON THEME SONG"

(Same as above; however, during the song, **TROUBLE** *breaks away from the group and tiptoes out of sight.)*

*(***ESTHER*** *smashes the alarm clock to punctuate the end of the song. Everyone bows and goes back to sleep.)*

(Pause. Day becomes night, almost becomes day, but holds in the dim…)

NEXT…

Prologue "Theft"

(Everyone is still sleeping.)

*(**TROUBLE** sneaks into the space, he tiptoes carefully in an over-exaggerated fashion past the sleeping characters. He cautiously approaches the chair. He reaches out tentatively for the hammer, but the **ROCKSTAR** rolls over in his sleep causing **TROUBLE** to leap back. He regains his composure and again approaches the chair. This time he touches the hammer. As his hand makes contact, a warm spotlight appears and a choir begins to sing. **TROUBLE** pulls his hand back, but no one rouses. He tries again and it happens again just the same. One last time and **TROUBLE** takes the hammer.)*

*(The music fades, but the spot follows him as he begins to sneak away. He notices the light following him and tries to shoe it away. It moves away, but then chases him down again. He tries to identify the source of the light, but can't see past the glare. In searching for the light source, **TROUBLE** becomes conscious of the audience. He looks around awkwardly trying to hide the hammer behind his back. Taking the audience in, he reveals the hammer, shows it to the audience. He locks his arms in the air holding the hammer high and two more spots click onto him with a loud locking noise as all other light vanishes. In the three spots, with the hammer held high, he clears his throat…)*

TROUBLE. I have an announcement…

(pause)

Okay, okay, okay, um, okay: I have an announcement. And I guess, I guess this is it:

(He clears his throat.)

For too long we have been captive to the will of a dictator! To these whims, these flights of fancy. I ask you, what is there to be afraid of here, except what she says should be frightening? Why is change so threatening?

Everything here is soft and fun and exciting. Just like this, over and over and over, everyone asleep, up to perform, back to sleep. The insidious tedium and monotony eating away at our freedoms.

We do what we're told, we do what we're told. Ideas, an idea like a poison, slowly seeping into everything. Into you, into you. Into me… but not anymore! Might does not make right! I say the time has come for change! And this…

(He presents the hammer…)

This is the agent of change. Or, I guess more accurately, I am the agent of change and this is the vehicle. Oh yeah. So I say down with the popular authority! No more consequences, no more law! No more fear! No more damned theme songs! Now is the time to rise up!

(He blushes slightly.)

Um…but don't tell anyone you saw me, okay?

*(The general lights return abruptly and the spotlights fade away. **TROUBLE** clutches the hammer to his chest and hastily exits.)*

NEXT…

Episode I "Something's Missing"

(The alarm clock goes off. It rattles on the table, a deafening ring. Everyone covers their ears or heads groaning as **ESTHER** *gropes around for her hammer. It has been taken. She panics, looking everywhere to no avail. Eventual, she throws a blanket on top of the clock, silencing it temporarily.)*

(She looks around for the hammer. Finding nothing, she rushes to the rope, climbs into the ceiling and disappears. Suddenly, she hangs down from the ceiling holding a huge, old-fashioned microphone.)

ESTHER. Wake up! Wake up! <<Wake up!>>

(The sleeping characters leap to their feet disoriented.)

We are now in a <<state of emergency!>>

WINSTON PUPPET. What [happened?]

AKANE. [What's] [going on?]

ESTHER. [<<Quiet!>>]

The hammer has been stolen. The small hammer has been stolen. I need for you to find it. Do you understand what I'm telling you? <<Do you?>>

YUMI. *(still half asleep)* But I wanna' go back to sleep.

(All of the other characters gasp sharply.)

ESTHER. Excuse me?

YUMI. I wanna' go…I mean, I mean [nothing.]

AKANE. [She didn't] say anything.

ESTHER. Listen to me, all of you: How can we sleep without the hammer? Who will stop the clock? It doesn't make sense! We can't just leave a blanket on the clock, that's not how things work. That's ridiculous, a blanket on a clock, just look at it…

(They all look with very disappointed gazes at the blanket-covered clock.)

And you all know, it's a pretty hammer, big and pretty and strong and hard and mine! <<MINE!>> You'll find it, you'll do what I say, you'll do it now, you'll do it fast and you'll do it because I say so. But mostly you'll do it because I'll be watching you and if you don't, much worse things will happen, things that you can't imagine, so I won't even try to describe, the kind of things that will make your ears scream just from hearing them. But in case you need a refresher…

(A series of slides rapidly play on the wall, varied images of extreme torture, but all being performed on a stick figure cartoon. There is an audible reaction from the assembled group upon viewing the images.)

ROCKSTAR. Rahr.

ESTHER. So sad. Is that what you want? <<Is it?>> I know you understand. Now…find the hammer!

(pause)

<<Find it!!!>>

*(**TROUBLE** scampers into view. He waves enthusiastically at everyone, holding the hammer in plain view. The **SCHOOL GIRLS** point to him…)*

YUMI. I found it.

AKANE. No, I found it.

YUMI. No, I [did!]

AKANE. [You] are such a liar.

YUMI. Uh uh, no way. It's totally right there.

AKANE. That's what I said!

YUMI. Shut-up!

AKANE. Shut-up!

ESTHER. *(pelting the **SCHOOL GIRLS** with small stuffed animals.)* <<Shut-up!>>

TROUBLE. Are you looking for me?

ESTHER. That's my Hammer!

TROUBLE. This?

ESTHER. <<Get him!>>

*(As the characters begin to converge on him, **TROUBLE** swings the hammer, smashing it into the ground. A deafening boom fills the space and everyone falls to the ground and **ESTHER** falls out of view. **TROUBLE** rushes off laughing. Everyone recovers, looks around and then they all rush off in different directions. The **SCHOOL GIRLS** remain…)*

NEXT…

Episode II "Truth in Advertising"

(The **GIRLS** *drift towards the now-covered alarm clock.)*

AKANE. I hate how she's [so…]

YUMI. [Wait.]

(They stop and look into the ceiling. There is no evidence that **ESTHER** *is present.)*

YUMI. Okay.

AKANE. I hate how she's so bossy. "Do this, find that!"

YUMI. I know, so pushy.

AKANE. You know, I was thinking the other day…

YUMI. Oh!

AKANE. Uh huh, I was. I was thinking about how lucky we are to live in such a beautiful place.

YUMI. We are lucky.

AKANE. And I was thinking that even though she's always bossing us around and yelling into that stupid microphone thing, we still get all the new movies at the mall, we get all the new fashions and my magazines always come on time.

YUMI. We should go to the mall.

AKANE. But if we can't enjoy all that stuff, then is it really so great?

YUMI. But I do enjoy that stuff.

AKANE. Hmmm, me too. But I still have to think about things I don't want. Like things that aren't fun or [interesting…]

YUMI. [Are you] talking about that hammer?

AKANE. Like that hammer is so important. Big deal.

YUMI. *(motioning to the blanket-covered clock)* I bet everything's fine under there.

AKANE. I bet it doesn't even work.

YUMI. I bet you're right.

WINSTON PUPPET. I don't think you should be near that.

AKANE. Did you hear something?

YUMI. *(pointedly turning to the* **WINSTON PUPPET** *…)* No.

AKANE. I dare you to look.

YUMI. I don't know…

AKANE. I double dare you!

> (**YUMI** *smiles broadly and pulls the blanket off the clock. The cacophonous ringing immediately returns. The* **SCHOOL GIRLS** *panic and throw the blanket back onto the clock.* **ESTHER** *hangs down from the ceiling in a rage.)*

ESTHER. *(Pelting the* **SCHOOL GIRLS** *with small stuffed animals.)* What are you doing? <<GO!>>

YUMI. [Ow!]

AKANE. [We have] to go to [school!]

YUMI. [Stop it!]

> (*The* **SCHOOL GIRLS** *rush off.* **ESTHER** *disappears back into the ceiling.)*

NEXT…

Episode III "Love Birds"

*(The **DAMSEL** is searching the stage for the hammer; looking around and under things, audience members, etc.)*

*(The **SUITOR** enters with some stealth. He has something behind his back. He sneaks up behind the **DAMSEL** and taps her on the shoulder. She is surprised, but seems happy to see him. He produces a bomb from behind his back, a circular black ball with a lit fuse. He offers it to her.)*

(She blushes and giggles, but declines in a courtly manner as if unable to accept the gift. However, she is clearly flattered. He throws the bomb off stage while walking away. He sits across the stage pouting.)

*(After a moment, a loud explosion comes from off stage. It draws the **DAMSEL**'s attention for only the briefest moment until she returns to searching. The **SUITOR** doesn't notice.)*

(The APPLAUSE sign flashes.)

*(Smoke pours on from where the bomb exploded and the **SCHOOL GIRLS** enter coughing.)*

YUMI. What was that about? I can't believe it just blew up like that.

AKANE. I know! Good thing we weren't actually in the school. That would have been bad.

WINSTON PUPPET. Are you two okay?

*(The **SCHOOL GIRLS** look at the **WINSTON PUPPET** and then at each other, confused…)*

YUMI. Are you talking to us?

AKANE. You're not talking to us are you?

YUMI. He's NOT talking to us.

WINSTON PUPPET. I just wanted to make sure you're [all right?]

YUMI. [Oh my] God, I hate smoke. It's so…smoky.

AKANE. Your hair still looks good though.

YUMI. Does it?

AKANE. Totally.

YUMI. Thanks.

AKANE. I mean, you use so much product.

YUMI. What?

AKANE. Oh no, I mean in a good way.

YUMI. Sure, it would take more than an explosion, right?

(They continue off, laughing…)

*(The **SUITOR** runs off; then enters again. He has something behind his back. He sneaks up behind the **DAMSEL** and taps her on the shoulder. She is again surprised, but again seems happy to see him. He produces a bomb from behind his back, some sticks of dynamite wrapped together with a ticking timer. He offers it to her.)*

(She again blushes and giggles, but declines in a courtly manner as if unable to accept the gift. Again, she is clearly flattered. He again throws the bomb off stage while walking away. He sits across the stage pouting.)

*(After a moment, a loud explosion comes from off stage. It draws the **DAMSEL**'s attention for only the briefest moment until she returns to searching. The **SUITOR** doesn't notice.)*

(The APPLAUSE sign flashes.)

*(Smoke pours on from where the bomb exploded and **TROUBLE** enters coughing. The **DAMSEL** and **SUITOR** perk up when they see him. He runs. They chase him off.)*

NEXT…

Episode IV "Show"

WINSTON PUPPET. Everything here's not what it seems. That's important to know. That's important to tell you so you don't get confused. But I guess I don't know, I don't know what to tell you. About this place. About me. About how I feel. My feelings about things. How do describe a feeling really? I mean really. Those fleeting things, you know? Hard to pin down in all the delicate, blunt, slippery, numbing movement. There's any number of words, but they all "feel" a bit off. But for the sake of argument, I'll try my best.

(clutching an oversized Thesaurus…)

Lament is an entirely appropriate word. I lament my current predicament. Although, it doesn't describe my general state, my larger condition, my ordeal. Hmmm... maybe…depressed? That's very clinical… that comes with associations that I'm not comfortable with, no, not depressed. And if anyone asks, it's not depression. My complaints are far more…precise. Maybe despair…in knowing oneself. That's good. Well no, not good but… or ennui…

(He sighs deeply.)

Ennui.

(He thinks for a moment…)

Ennui is absolutely the right word.

*(Pause. **ESTHER** hangs down from the ceiling with her microphone in hand.)*

ESTHER. <<Debris clean-up at the former school site! Hammer still missing. >> And now…a song. Brought to you by the proud employees of Watashi Heavy Industries. Happily binging you clean, wind-powered turbine energy, sleek refrigerators and home-use robots.

*(Lights shut out and a spot comes up on the **WINSTON PUPPET**. The schoolgirls and the male and female lovers rush in and sit at his feet with anticipation.)*

*(**WINSTON PUPPET** sighs deeply again. Then sings a ballad and does a little dance, soft-shoe style...)*

(As he finishes, the entire cast sighs deeply in unison.)

(The APPLAUSE sign flashes.)

WINSTON PUPPET. It's all really sad, you know?

ESTHER. Lights!

*(The lights return to reveal that **TROUBLE** is present among the characters enjoying the song. He leaps up, hammer in hand.)*

<<There he is!!!>>

*(As the characters rise to chase him, **TROUBLE** slams the hammer down with a deafening boom, knocking every-one to their feet. He exits quickly. Everyone rushes after him, the **SUITOR** is the last to leave...)*

WINSTON PUPPET. Wait! Yes, you, wait just a moment.

*(The **SUITOR** returns for a moment.)*

Listen, listen...okay, perhaps you've noticed I'm in a bit of a predicament.

(He shakes his arms and legs to make the ropes move.)

I can't do much of anything, can't go anywhere, even right over there. I'm immobile. And I thought perhaps you could help me? And of course, I could repay the favor. Uh huh, I've been watching you with your lady friend. I know a thing or two about the ladies and I could maybe offer you a bit of advice? What do you think of that?

*(The **SUITOR** seems unsure.)*

I guarantee you she'll love you. All you have to do is help me out.

*(The **SUITOR** nods in agreement, then crosses his arms and waits...)*

All right then, okay, I'll go first. Then I'll just trust you to keep up your end of the bargain. Now should I put this, hmmm, well, okay, I've noticed that you have a very "interesting" sense of what a woman might like, gift-wise I mean.

(*The* **SUITOR** *nods enthusiastically.*)

Oh no, no, you see, I'm saying that you should maybe try something else. Something, maybe, sweeter? Oh, all right, let's ask some actual women. Well, girls anyway…

(*The* **SCHOOL GIRLS** *cross the stage in conversation.*)

YUMI. Why does she even call it the small hammer?

AKANE. I know, it looked pretty big to me.

YUMI. Exactly. It's huge.

AKANE. It's just confusing.

WINSTON PUPPET. Excuse me? Excuse me for a moment?

YUMI. Um…are you talking to us?

WINSTON PUPPET. Yes, I was wondering if you might answer a question for us, a very quick question?

AKANE. I think he's talking to us.

YUMI. What is it?

WINSTON PUPPET. Hypothetically, if a boy gave [you…]

AKANE. [Hypo]-what?

WINSTON PUPPET. Oh it means not [necessarily…]

YUMI. [She's making] fun of you. She knows what it means.

(*They giggle.*)

WINSTON PUPPET. Oh, well, if a boy, hypothetically, gave you a bomb for a present, would you like it?

AKANE. That's such an insensitive question.

YUMI. Our school just blew up. Right there.

AKANE. I can't even believe you. We're really upset about it.

YUMI. It happened right there.

AKANE. So insensitive.

(*The* **SCHOOL GIRLS** *cross to another area and sit down. They both open pop-star magazines and begin reading.*)

WINSTON PUPPET. Okay, well, bad example, but really you might try something else. I really think it might go over better, win her a little faster if you will. Sometimes women can be fickle, sometimes you have to try a different approach to get through all of their defenses.

(The **SUITOR** *shrugs.)*

I would try flowers. Some nice flowers. Maybe even roses, if that's not too passé. Roses are beautiful really and they have a longstanding recognition as a symbol of love.

(The **SUITOR** *lights up. He is pleased.)*

Good?

(The **SUITOR** *nods in the affirmative.)*

Now you'll help me? All I want you to do is unhook these ropes so that I can experience some freedom, something different than this same old thing day after day. Can you do that?

(The **SUITOR** *obliges, unhooking the ropes, the* **WINSTON PUPPET** *then falls against the wall, slumped on the ground. He is now unable to move at all.)*

Thank you. This so unexpected; this feeling of weightlessness. This feeling of...um, could you sit me up against the wall please?

(The **SUITOR** *does this. The* **WINSTON PUPPET**'s *head lolls to one side, but he seems happy.)*

(The **SUITOR** *exits.)*

It's like a whole new world.

(He sighs deeply. **TROUBLE** *runs on with the hammer...)*

TROUBLE. And that's what we're looking for ladies and gentlemen.

(He slams the hammer down knocking everyone down.)

NEXT...

Episode V "Rockstar Sighting"

*(The **SCHOOL GIRLS** are on stage. Recovering from being knocked down.)*

AKANE. Dammit!

YUMI. I wish he'd stop doing that.

AKANE. Are you okay?

YUMI. Uh huh.

(The lights pulse and dim.)

(The APPLAUSE sign flashes.)

*(The **ROCKSTAR** enters and the sound of thunderous applause is heard. The **SCHOOL GIRLS** drop their magazines in awe. He crosses the stage waving to people, raising his arms up in triumph as an insane amount of flash bulbs go off and the sound of photographs rises through the crown noise. As he exits, the photographs stop, the applause dies away and the **SCHOOL GIRLS** are left alone again.)*

YUMI. He was so [cute.]

AKANE. [SO] cute!

YUMI. I know, [I just said…]

AKANE. [I mean,] just really cute!

YUMI. Okay I think I get that he was cute, I said he was cute first.

AKANE. Sorry.

YUMI. It's okay. I'm sorry for being snippy.

(They hug.)

AKANE. You're wearing really pretty eye shadow. It works nicely. I can't wait to ask him out.

YUMI. Thanks you're lip gloss is…wait, what?

AKANE. I can't wait to ask [him out.]

YUMI. [I heard what] you said, you can't ask him out. He loves me. It's so totally obvious.

AKANE. Oh see, and I thought it was pretty blatant that he clearly loves me.

YUMI. What are you [talking about???]

AKANE. [We can just] decide to disagree okay?

    (Pause. She hugs **YUMI**…*)*

YUMI. Okay. I'm sorry.

AKANE. It's okay.

YUMI. Isn't funny, I don't know what came over me, really. Such a bizarre thing.

AKANE. Yes, bizarre. I can't even put it into words. But you know, I'm not really good at that stuff. Word stuff.

YUMI. Me either. And maybe it's more than words could handle. More [than…]

AKANE. [Ha! It] makes me blush though. When I think of him. It makes me, I don't know, [silly.]

YUMI. [Me too.] Just the same.

AKANE. Just the same?

YUMI. But I mean…well, it was exciting how he, you have to admit that he was staring at me.

AKANE. I think he was staring at you. But only so it wouldn't be obvious that his love for me is virtually overwhelming his senses.

YUMI. That doesn't make sense. He was staring at me.

AKANE. That's what I said. You know nothing about boys. It's sad.

    (YUMI *slaps* **AKANE** *in the face. Pause.)*

    Really?

YUMI. I'm sorry.

AKANE. It's okay. We all get a little carried away sometimes.

YUMI. I know but I'm so sorry, does it hurt.

AKANE. Yes, but not as bad as this one time I remember. We were running to catch the bus and I slipped. It was raining and I slipped. Remember that? And you stopped, we were both soaking wet, but you stopped to help me up, but I had that really deep cut on my knee and it was bleeding everywhere and you said we should…

(She abruptly punches **YUMI** *in the face, knocking her to the ground.)*

You said we should call the doctor. That time totally hurt more than this.

YUMI. Huh? I don't remember that.

AKANE. Oh... um, maybe that was someone else. Sorry. It's [just that...]

YUMI. [You can't] have him, I saw him [first.]

AKANE. [Just try] and stop me....

YUMI. Come back here!

(She chases **AKANE** *off...)*

NEXT...

Episode VI "Briefly"

(**TROUBLE** *is sneaking across the stage with the hammer. The spotlights reappear with the locking noise again taking him off-guard. He composes himself and holds the hammer firmly in front of his chest as he speaks…*)

TROUBLE. Okay, okay, okay, um…okay. Things are going well. Or at least…um, thing are going…

(Pause. He relaxes a bit.)

I mean, things are happening at least. And my methods for mixing up this crazy, not-too-far fetched totalitarian state haven't resulted in any serious damage to this point. I mean, no one's been hurt or anything. Accept for that school full of children that blew up. But that totally happened where you couldn't see it, so it doesn't matter.

You don't know how it is here, how could you, right? It's the same every day. We wake up, we do mindless things to keep us entertained and distracted. We follow the occasional directive from above.

(He sticks his tongue out in the direction of the ceiling.)

Nothing means anything. And it's always the same. And that damn theme song. Jeez.

WINSTON PUPPET. Excuse me.

(A spotlight rises on the **WINSTON PUPPET.***)*

Excuse me, I'm sorry to interrupt. Persuasive stuff.

TROUBLE. Thanks.

WINSTON PUPPET. I was just wondering, how do you know that's bad?

TROUBLE. What?

WINSTON PUPPET. Everything being the same every day, how do you know things might not be worse if they changed? Sometimes when things change, they aren't what you expected. How do you know it won't be worse?

TROUBLE. I don't know. I just do.

WINSTON PUPPET. Youthful idealism.

TROUBLE. Maybe. But that kinda' makes me sound flighty. I'm instigating a revolution here.

WINSTON PUPPET. Hang on to that for as long as you can.

TROUBLE. *(With a big smile…)* I'll try.

WINSTON PUPPET. Okay, I'll let you get back to your propaganda.

TROUBLE. Thanks. Wait… it's not propaganda. What I'm saying is the truth.

WINSTON PUPPET. Same thing maybe?

TROUBLE. No.

WINSTON PUPPET. Or perspective maybe?

TROUBLE. I don't [think…]

WINSTON PUPPET. [It depends] who's listening maybe?

TROUBLE. Wait, what do [you mean?]

WINSTON PUPPET. [No, no, no,] I'm sure you're right. The truth is the truth. I'm sorry I interrupted. Please continue.

(The WINSTON PUPPET *sighs deeply as his light disappears.)*

TROUBLE. I'll keep saying it: things need to change. No one seems to understand, we don't have to exist in a culture of fear all the time. No one's gonna' get hurt. Well…

(He looks toward where the school exploded…)

None of the main players anyway.

(The general light returns abruptly and the spotlights fade as he makes his way off stage.)

NEXT…

Episode XXVIII "Ideal Future"

(**ESTHER** *is perched above. She lights a Hookah and inhales deeply. As she exhales a cloud of smoke [from Orange flavored tobacco] over the stage, the lights shift to a new orange glow and a softness descends over the proceedings.*)

ESTHER. Sometimes a promise of what will be is just that. Sometimes it's enough to keep you occupied. Sometimes it's enough to keep the status quo. The way things are, a promise of what things will be…

This glimpse of the future is brought to you by Shipbuilding & Ocean Development Headquarters, a division of Watashi Heavy Industries. Bringing you tankers, carriers, cruise ships and special-purpose sea vessels, including military defense submersibles, all designed to make life better.

(*She takes another long drag and exhales. All of the characters appear on stage…*)

TROUBLE. I want someone to give me a place where we can speak our minds freely.

YUMI. I want someone [to give me…]

AKANE. [I want someone] to give me…

ESTHER. Yes.

WINSTON PUPPET. I want to go wherever I, wherever we want to go…

TROUBLE. Freely.

WINSTON PUPPET. Whenever we want to go.

ROCKSTAR. Rahr.

WINSTON PUPPET. Without limits and [boundaries and…]

AKANE. [Without all] the bombs and [stuff.]

YUMI. [At least] not at our [school.]

AKANE. [At least] not in my head.

YUMI. Do you think I could have a hamster that doesn't sleep all the time?

AKANE. Yes, and he'll love you so much.

DAMSEL. *(very quietly…)* And he'll love me so much.

YUMI. [And my parents?]

AKANE. [And my parents?]

ESTHER. Yes.

WINSTON PUPPET. And maybe a new place to sit, when I want to sit.

DAMSEL. *(very quietly…)* And he'll love me so much.

WINSTON PUPPET. Where people [will notice me.]

AKANE. [Where people] [will notice me.]

TROUBLE. [Where people] won't notice me.

ROCKSTAR. Rahr.

TROUBLE. Even if I want them to [notice me.]

YUMI. [I want to] notice things more.

TROUBLE. Because I don't really want them to [notice me.]

YUMI. [Let things] impact me.

DAMSEL. *(very quietly…)* And he will.

ESTHER. Yes.

AKANE. And a new zipper toggle [for my bag.]

YUMI. [And a new] hair brush when my [hair get crazy.]

AKANE. [And a new] brain, to think new ways about stuff.

YUMI. And a new heart, [so I can feel again a little.]

WINSTON PUPPET. [So I can feel again a little.]

TROUBLE. More than a hammer swing, feel [more than a…]

AKANE. [More than a] bruise on my hand, feel [more than a…]

YUMI. [More than a] punch in the face, feel [more than a…]

AKANE. [More than an] explosion behind my back, feel [more than a…]

WINSTON PUPPET. [More than a] pain from nothing, feel [more than a…]

TROUBLE. [More than an] angry need for motion, feel more than…

DAMSEL. *(very quietly…)* He will love me so much.

ROCKSTAR. *(very quietly…)* Rahr.

> *(Lights fade on the stage leaving only **ESTHER** illuminated in a cloud of smoke. A moment that's almost serene…)*

ESTHER. And sometimes a promise is just that, nothing but a promise.
<<NEXT!>>

NEXT…

Episode VII "Love Birds 2"

*(The **DAMSEL** is still searching the stage for the hammer; looking around and under things, audience members, etc. She seems almost dizzy with the effort.)*

*(The **SUITOR** enters yet again with some stealth. He has something behind his back. He sneaks up behind the **DAMSEL** and taps her on the shoulder. She is surprised, but seems happy to see him. He produces a bouquet of flowers, bends down on one knee and offers it to her.)*

*(She looks confused and very serious. She slowly reaches out and takes the bouquet from the **SUITOR**. He seems blissfully happy. He places his hands over his heart in a gesture of love. She looks away, still troubled. In one swift motion she draws a gun and shoots the Suitor dead, all the while focusing on the flowers with her look of confusion.)*

(The APPLAUSE sign flashes.)

*(The **SUITOR** lays still, dead and bleeding among the stuffed animals and toys. **ESTHER** hangs down from the ceiling…)*

ESTHER. What are you doing? Why are you shooting people? <<We need as many people as we can get to look for my hammer.>> Did you hear me? Get back to looking! <<Get moving!>>

*(**ESTHER** pelts the **DAMSEL** with small stuffed toys. She does not move for a moment, continuing to stare at the flowers. Eventually, she slowly walks off stage, inhaling deeply from the bouquet along the way.)*

And now, an educational outreach, a minor distraction, a brief history of the political landscape:

(The lights shut out and slides again appear on the wall. This time they are shots of different characters, they are all post-assassination photos.)

Many years ago, we were a disorganized band of towns. Very tribal, very raw. This loose association of communities was unified by Bolinger the Duck. Bolinger was killed by a foreign power and leadership fell to Unti-lololo. But no one could understand anything he said; therefore, he was quickly killed and a rapid succession of leaders followed: Chihuli DeMan, Smirky, Fini Fini, but order was restored by the local chapter 273 of the society of machete wielding acrobats. Good people. They were fairly stable and everyone was pretty happy with the government, unfortunately a power mad dictator assassinated all of the members of chapter 273. The most controlling, nightmarish and destructive force that we've ever seen: <<Cynthia.>>

(She pauses for dramatic effect.)

Cynthia ruled with an iron fist for a long time and public executions were a pretty common Sunday outing. But that's no way to live and several factions tried to eliminate Cynthia. However, they were all defeated and subjected to the worst punishments imaginable. It's only recently she was overthrown, in a military insurgency... by me.

(A smiling photo of **ESTHER** *is the final slide.)*

So people disagree about how exactly a government should work. That gave us Bolinger the Duck, Untilololo, Chihuli DeMan, Smirky, Fini Fini, local chapter 273 of the machete wielding acrobats, Cynthia and me. Because really, people are fickle.

I should say, I think the idea of violence, the fear of it, is a much better motivator than actual violence. That is, in my opinion, where a lot of folks get tripped up. Like Cynthia. Don't get me wrong; I'm totally in favor of hurting people when you need to. <<Just so now you know.>>

(The lights return to normal.)

NEXT...

Episode VIII "Like young girls do…"

(The **SCHOOL GIRLS** *are on stage.)*

AKANE. About earlier…?

YUMI. I don't know what I was thinking.

AKANE. I don't know what I was doing.

YUMI. I just had this crazy feeling when I saw him.

AKANE. I know, me too. I know.

YUMI. Didn't we do this?

AKANE. What we're doing now?

YUMI. Apologies and bad with words and blushes.

AKANE. Did we do this? Blushes, yes, I remember that.

YUMI. Look, I'm just sorry is all.

AKANE. I know, me too. Really.

YUMI. Oh, look at that.

AKANE. Hmmm.

YUMI. Looks like someone got shot.

AKANE. Ick! He's bleeding all over the place.

YUMI. I wonder if anyone found that stupid hammer thing?

WINSTON PUPPET. Nope, still no hammer.

AKANE. That was rhetorical.

YUMI. Don't encourage him.

AKANE. I'm too nice sometimes, I know. I just feel bad for people.

YUMI. I understand. And why is he on the ground now anyway?

AKANE. Isn't that where he was before?

(The lights pulse and dim.)

(The APPLAUSE sign flashes.)

(The **ROCKSTAR** *enters and the sound of thunderous applause is heard. He crosses the stage waving to people, raising his arms up in triumph as an insane amount of flash bulbs go off and the sound of photographs rises through the crown noise. As he exits, the photographs*

stop, the applause dies away and the **SCHOOL GIRLS** *are left alone again. During the following transaction, their attention remains fixed on where the* **ROCKSTAR** *exited.)*

AKANE. There are no words to describe how amazing he is!

YUMI. Beautiful.

AKANE. Stunning.

YUMI. Handsome.

AKANE. Famous.

YUMI. Brilliant.

AKANE. Breathtaking.

YUMI. No words to describe him. No words [at all.]

AKANE. [I'm really] glad we've decided not to fight over him.

YUMI. Me too.

AKANE. Because our friendship is better than that.

YUMI. Uh huh. And you know I love you, right?

AKANE. Uh huh. Me too.

(Pause. The girls look at each other and immediately descend into a blood sport death match that includes: slapping, wrestling, tearing of clothing, pulling of hair, punching, kicking and biting.)

YUMI. Wait, wait! What are we doing?

AKANE. What?

YUMI. What are we doing?

AKANE. I don't…I don't know. I don't even know.

YUMI. This is just crazy. I don't want to fight with you.

AKANE. Oh, I don't want to fight with you either.

YUMI. I love you.

AKANE. I love you too.

(They hug.)

YUMI. So does that mean, what does that mean?

AKANE. Well I mean…

(A flurry of screaming, bloody violence ensues. Eventually Yumi chokes Akane to death.)

(The APPLAUSE sign flashes.)

YUMI. *(Wiping the blood and hair from her face…)* You're my best friend.

(She rushes after the **ROCKSTAR.** *)*

NEXT…

Episode IX "Show"

*(The **DAMSEL** wanders on with the flowers. She drops them at the **SUITOR'**s side. She sits up his dead body and tries to make him hold the flowers. It is difficult.)*

WINSTON PUPPET. It's hard without ropes. They make things easier. I used to have ropes. Those were the days. Things were so much better then I think.

(She moves his arms around.)

See what I mean.

(She nods.)

You should get ready. It's almost time I think.

(She looks around.)

Almost time.

*(The **DAMSEL** rises, she is still holding the flowers.)*

ESTHER. <<Relevant body count stands at two! Hammer still missing. >> And now… dance. This dance is sponsored by Paper & Printing, suppliers of pulp, conversion and extrusion machinery and an invaluable part of the Watashi Heavy Industries team.

*(The spotlight appears on the **WINSTON PUPPET** again, now leaning against the wall. A second spot appears on the **DAMSEL**. As the **WINSTON PUPPET** begins to sing a classic slow dance as the **DAMSEL** desperately tries to lift the **SUITOR** to dance with her, but he is too heavy and she can barely maneuver him before he falls into a pile on the ground again.)*

*(She is clearly losing it. She turns on the audience surveying them. She desperately selects a male audience member and drags him up to dance with her. The **VOLUNTEER** does his best, but she is crying and falling apart. She abandons the **VOLUNTEER** and returns to the side of the **SUITOR** crying. She begins to lose control. Her attention focuses towards the **WINSTON PUPPET** who continues singing, oblivious.)*

(She pulls out her gun and shoots him dead. She then turns on the **VOLUNTEER**, *laughing through tears, and shoots him as well. He is sent spinning with a spray of blood to the floor.)*

(The APPLAUSE sign flashes.)

(She is still laughing when she rushes from the stage.)

ESTHER. <<End of dance.>>

(Lights return to normal. **ESTHER** *disappears again into the ceiling. The bodies remain on stage.)*

NEXT…

Episode XXIX "More Probable Future"

*(**ESTHER** is holding the hookah. The soft orange light begins to return and the remaining cast members begin to emerge onto stage…)*

ESTHER. So like I said, sometimes a promise is just a promise. And sometimes people will believe just to believe. And sometimes…if I show where that promise will really take you…?

This glimpse into the future is brought to you by everyone at Guided Weapon Systems, a division of Watashi Heavy Industries. Serving all of your Surface to Air ASM-2, SSM-1, AAM-3 and Type 97 Torpedo wants and needs with a smile.

(Pause. The characters finish assembling.)

You might not like it.

(Blackout. All of the characters scream in the dark. As in severe physical pain. The screams grow to a cacophonous level and then fade to just the sound of a few isolated whimpers and sobs.)

NEXT…

Episode X "Candid Moments"

(The lights rise abruptly and **TROUBLE** *is standing on stage with the* **DAMSEL, ROCKSTAR** *and* **YUMI.** *They chase him around the set and a searchlight crosses the stage. As each one of the characters pass through the light, the other characters freeze in place and we catch a glimpse, a pause to reflect on their inner thoughts.)*

YUMI. I really hope we have everything in common. After we find this stupid hammer we can spend all kinds of quality time together. I bet he likes all the same bands I do. I bet his favorite color is green, just like mine. He's so beautiful. I wonder what my best friend would be thinking now? He's gonna' be mine.

TROUBLE. I'm right. Right? I have to be right. Right? No questions. Right.

ROCKSTAR. *(sweetly…)* People have the wrong idea bout me. For whatever reason, they're really drawn to me. I think it's because I don't really talk much. Mostly, I just say "rahr." I have kind of different ways of saying it…

(He demonstrates the different ways he says "rahr.")

But it's pretty much just "rahr." And people can read whatever they want into that, ya' know? And when I say people, I really mean you. And so people tend to think very highly of me and want to be around me.

(An explosion of flash bulbs fills the room and a thunderous round of applause.)

People like me. So when I turn on them, it always seems to come as a surprise. It's funny, how they always look surprised, even though I have these big claws and they don't really know me. But that's all about what we allow ourselves to believe about other people. And when I say ourselves, I really mean you.

They get panicked, you know? If they're not expecting it. If you run right towards them, they don't usually run away. No, they just kind of stand there with this look on their face like… "I can't believe this is happening."

Which is kinda' funny, right? Because they should really run away. 'Cause the idea of being hurt, what you maybe think that's like is nowhere near as bad as it actually is when you get hurt. And if you ever get hurt, that's when you know. It's hard to remember though, what that feels like, 'cause it's so foreign, ya' know? So then, everybody's fight of flight response gets all mixed up and they end up just standing there.

(pause)

Waiting for it.

That's the thing about people. They're not often too quick on their feet, with their wits, when it comes down to it. They'll just sit there and take it, whatever it is, before they even realize they might not deserve it. And when I say people, I really mean you.

Listen, I have a strong track record of mauling everyone that I'm around for any decent amount of time.

I mean, I guess this is kinda' a life lesson, ya' know? So remember this: if I'm running towards you, well, you know…run away. Don't worry; when the time comes you won't remember that. You'll just stand there. Waiting for it.

*(As the light catches the **DAMSEL**, **YUMI** and **ROCKSTAR** chase **TROUBLE** off the stage leaving her alone…)*

DAMSEL. *(quietly through tears…)* He loves me, he loves me not, he loves me, he loves me not, he loves me, he loves me not…

(The light fades to dim as she drifts from the stage.)

NEXT…

Episode XI "Getting to know you..."

(The **ROCKSTAR** *and* **YUMI** *sit next to each other. Much like a first date. There is an explosion of photo bulbs flashing and audience applause initially. It fades away as the two sit awkwardly.)*

YUMI. So this is fun.

(awkward pause)

I was so glad you were interested in me. I know that sounds a bit forward, but it really did make me happy. I wanted you to know.

(awkward pause)

Do you like my hair?

(Pause. The **ROCKSTAR** *shrugs.)*

Oh, you know my school exploded. Right over there. Some kind of bombing.

(pause)

I know; I didn't really care either.

(long awkward pause)

So you don't talk much do you?

(The **ROCKSTAR** *shakes his head no.)*

But you're famous and attractive and popular. So that's good.

ROCKSTAR. Rahr.

YUMI. I think that's good.

ROCKSTAR. Rahr.

YUMI. You know what? I miss my friend. I wish she could have been here with us. You really would have liked her I think. We always had things to talk about. She had great hair like me. She was fun and we would share the same lip gloss. We both liked cherry flavor. Do you wear lip gloss?

(pause)

YUMI. *(cont.)* No, I guess you wouldn't.

(*long pause*)

I miss her.

(*She takes* **ROCKSTAR**'*s hand. Lights fade again to dim in an explosion of flash bulbs and the loudest canned audience applause yet.*)

NEXT…

Episode XII "Show"

(Immediate spotlight on **ESTHER** *as she hangs down from the ceiling.)*

ESTHER. <<Body count is now four. Hammer still missing.>> And ladies and gentlemen, our featured entertainer seems to have suffered a minor career setback.

(Lights flicker briefly on the **WINSTON PUPPET** *'s body.)*

So now, and only as a last resort, brought to you by Watashi Heavy Industries Steel Structures & Construction Division if you need a suspension bridge or tunneling and foundation machinery, depend on Watashi. <<I offer you this…>>

(She proceeds to sing a torch ballad through her microphone. It is beautiful. The remaining characters drift onto stage looking up at her during the song. They are all crying.)

(The APPLAUSE sign flashes.)

(When she finishes, the spotlight shuts out abruptly with a locking noise. As the lights return to normal below.)

NEXT…

Episode XIII "Finale"

ESTHER. *(still in the calm manner, as if a tag on the song…)* <<Grab him. >>

YUMI. Gotcha!

*(The **ROCKSTAR** and **YUMI** grab **TROUBLE**. He tries to swing the hammer, but they are holding his arms tightly. **DAMSEL** holds him at gunpoint.)*

ROCKSTAR. Rahr.

TROUBLE. Let me go! You don't have to listen to her! It doesn't have [to be…]

ESTHER. [<<Shut-up.>>]

*(Lights immediately drop to dim as two floor-mounted spotlights illuminate one wall of the theatre. A gigantic banner unfurls down with the wall with a brave and glorious photo of **ESTHER** reminiscent of the Eastern European propaganda. **ESTHER** begins moving down the rope, returning to the ground while speaking…)*

I am sick and tired of your incessant whining and complaining about the state of our society. You have no idea what it takes to keep things, simple everyday things, basic day to day things, running smoothly. Just look at what's happened since you stole the small hammer. And now…

(She reaches the ground.)

Now I'm going to take my small hammer back and teach you a lesson.

TROUBLE. No!

*(He breaks loose and swings the hammer down with a deafening thud. The characters around him fall to the ground. **ESTHER** is not affected. Shocked, he swings the hammer again. Another deafening thud and the characters jerk on the ground, but **ESTHER** continues to move towards him. With a scream, she leaps at him. The grapple and roll, fighting for the hammer. **TROUBLE***

eventually breaks away from her and swings the hammer repeatedly, keeping her at bay.)

ESTHER. Give it back.

TROUBLE. I won't ever submit to your authority! Never again!!

ESTHER. Well I...

(Pause. Stand off.)

Well I'm sorry that you feel that way. But I'll just have to respect your opinions.

TROUBLE. What?

ESTHER. Contrary to your "inflammatory statements" this is not some kind of police state. You do have free will. Absolutely. You can make your own decisions and I will respect them. We all will respect them.

TROUBLE. *(looking as if he might cry...)* Really?

(She nods.)

Really?

ESTHER. I'm not as bad as all that. You just have to accept responsibility for your decisions. That's an integral part of being free, right?

TROUBLE. That makes sense.

ESTHER. Yes it does. Fair is fair. So you hang on to the hammer for now if that's what you want.

TROUBLE. And the theme song?

ESTHER. Well I am quite fond of that theme song. But...

(looking around...)

We'll need some new recruits I guess. So we'll take a little break on that as well.

TROUBLE. It's like a dream come true.

ESTHER. And I've even got one more special treat for you.

TROUBLE. What is it?

*(She claps her hands and the lights dim. A 1950s model television wrapped in chains descends from the sky. It's soft blue light emits an a glow. **TROUBLE** is transfixed*

by the screen. As it moves close enough, he reaches up and guides it to the floor, He cannot tear his eyes away.)

It's SOOOOO beautiful.

ESTHER. Isn't it?

TROUBLE. I love it.

ESTHER. I'm glad.

*(She snaps her fingers. The **DAMSEL** crosses over to them, still in her zombie-like daze, and nonchalantly executes **TROUBLE** by shooting him in the head.)*

(The APPLAUSE sign flashes.)

(ESTHER *stands over his body.)*

This is my world you ridiculous infant. What did you learn?

(She waits for an answer.)

That's what I thought.

(She regains her composure…)

Somebody get this thing out of here!

(The television ascends into the sky again.)

NEXT…

Epilogue "Bedtime"

(**YUMI**, **ROCKSTAR** *and* **DAMSEL** *stand together. They all look weary, exhausted even.*)

(**ESTHER** *picks up the small hammer. As she picks it up, the special light and music from the first scene return briefly. She pays them no mind.*)

ESTHER. It's time things got back to normal. I know it's been a very rough day for everyone. You've all put in a tremendous effort, nice work.

(*The three characters nod.*)

ROCKSTAR. Rahr.

YUMI. You can say that again.

ROCKSTAR. Rahr.

(*The* **DAMSEL** *raises the gun and points it at* **YUMI**…)

YUMI. What are you doing?

(*She shrugs.* **YUMI** *is annoyed.*)

Don't point that at me. What is she doing?

(*The* **DAMSEL** *shoots* **YUMI**. *She spins from the shot as blood sprays across the* **ROCKSTAR**.)

(*The APPLAUSE sign flashes.*)

ROCKSTAR. (*He touches her face with his claw…*) Rahr.

(*The* **DAMSEL** *takes aim at* **ROCKSTAR**. **ESTHER** *holds up her hand.*)

ESTHER. You really need to stop that now.

(*The* **DAMSEL** *lowers the gun.*)

There you go.

(*And then, very quietly…*)

DAMSEL. What am I doing?

(**ESTHER** *and* **ROCKSTAR** *both cock their heads, curious*)

ESTHER. You can talk?

DAMSEL. What am I even doing?

ESTHER. She can talk?

ROCKSTAR. Rahr?

DAMSEL. It's so much darker.

ESTHER. You know, I've never heard your voice before. I don't think I even knew you had one.

DAMSEL. This isn't... right.

ROCKSTAR. Rahr.

ESTHER. Shhhh, now, don't be silly. You'll get used to it. Anyone can get used to anything. You'd be amazed. You'll see.

(The **DAMSEL** *drops the gun. It really just falls from her hand. She is basically an empty shell at this point.)*

*(***ESTHER*** pulls the blanket back revealing the insanely loud alarm clock. It is still ringing.* **ROCKSTAR** *covers his ears. The* **DAMSEL** *continues to just stand there.)*

And now, ladies and gentlemen, let's get some sleep.

*(***ESTHER*** lifts the small hammer and smashes the clock in a cacophony of smashing noises.)*

(Lights black out, except for the two floor spots that keep the giant banner illuminated.)

(After a moment, the spot lights shut off abruptly with a loud locking noise.)

END

Also by
Steve Yockey...

Bright. Apple. Crush.

Large Animal Games

Octopus

Subculture

Please visit our website **samuelfrench.com** for complete
descriptions and licensing information.

OTHER TITLES AVAILABLE FROM SAMUEL FRENCH

LARGE ANIMAL GAMES

Steve Yockey

Comedy / 4m, 3f

This incisive, unexpected, and larger than life tale of sex, love, and self delusion tracks the overlapping escapades of a group of friends old enough to know better in love but still naïve enough to mess things up anyway, and the man who supplies them with equal parts tough love, lingerie and self awareness. In a series of fluid scenes, *Large Animal Games* takes a comically skewed and razor-sharp look at modern relationships through a mix of bullfights, big game hunting and intimate apparel.

"Yockey's plays frequently involve the human fascination with violence, self-destruction and other dark impulses, but *Large Animal Games* turns out to be his brightest and most open-hearted work, and even the bittersweet moments retain a generosity of spirit."
– Creative Loafing

"The play has a touch of the magical dimension familiar to audiences who saw [Yockey's] *Skin* or *Octopus*, but it operates here in a more lighthearted way, while still nicely augmenting the subtly related themes of animal-lust, competition, self-image and possesion cleverly at work under the frilly, scanty surface."
– San Francisco Bay Guardian

"We are all animals, according to Yockey. And as such, we're enslaved by our primal instincts. The characters in *Large animal Games* all desire intimacy or fulfillment, but they have different - sometimes bizarre - ways of seeking it."
– East Bay Express

"An engaging writer, particularly skillful in depicting the poignant comedy of lovers' misunderstandings"
– SF Chronicle

SAMUELFRENCH.COM